I0822558

You see my big toe? Believe it or not I almost lost it the other day! No joke! Mom says I'm just over reacting but I know what happened and it is the scariest thing I have ever gone through.

My name is Emma and I promise that the story I am about to tell you is the truth.

It all started about a week before my Martial Art School had its big belt test. "Attention students!" Master M. said. "Today we will be working on some Air Shield Drills. Everyone pair up and grab a shield."

I teamed up with Ethan as I always do. I don't mind and I don't think he does either. We are both the same size and we seem to work well together.

“OK belts I want to see power and lots of energy as you hit the shield!” Master M. said. “Make sure you not only punch but kick as well.”

The Air Shield is my favorite drill, and when Master M. told us to begin I started hitting the shield with all my might! I was on fire, knocking Ethan back with every hit. I went in
for a strong kick and when I hit the shield I felt as though something had stabbed my Big Toe with a knife.

When class ended I took my shoes and socks off to see if I had injured my big toe. I could see it was red on one side, and it hurt when I tried to touch it. I thought that I probably just had kicked wrong and that's why my toe was this way.

“Is something wrong, Emma?” Master M. asked. He was looking over my shoulder as I was crouched over my foot. “No sir.” I said “I thought I felt something in my sock is all.” I smiled and began to put my socks and shoes back on. I did not want to worry him because I was afraid he may not let me test.

When I got home I went to my room to figure out what I was going to do. Testing was in a few days and if my toe didn't get better, how would I be able to get through the test?

If I told my mom, would she keep me from testing? If I didn't tell anyone, would my toe get worse and fall off? I was going crazy not knowing what to do and that's when I heard that wicked laugh.

“MUUHAHAHAHAHA!” the sound filled my whole room. “Who’s there?” I said. “Smack Smack” the sound of lips smacking echoed all around me. I began to scream but nothing seemed to come out.

I just stood frozen in the middle of my room, unable to move. “MUAHAHAHAHA!” The sound came again and that’s when I realized where it was coming from. I stood there shocked as I saw the toenail on my big toe laughing right at me.

“My name is Ingrown, Ingrown Toenail to be exact. And I want to thank you for the toe.” He smiled at me with a mean look on his face.

“Thank me? What do you mean?” I replied.

With a cruel chuckle Ingrown replied, “Thank you for allowing me to eat the toe.”

‘EAT THE TOE?” I shouted! “MOOOOOOM!”

My mom came bursting into my room "Emma what's wrong? Are you OK?" She could see I was worried and came over to give me a hug.

"Well I was afraid to say anything, but the toenail on my big toe is ALIVE!"

"He calls himself Ingrown Toenail and says he's going to eat my big toe!" I showed my mom my big toe but the Evil Ingrown toenail had decided to hide his face.

My mom looked at me as if I had flowers coming out of my ears. “I don’t see anything, Emma, except some soreness around your toenail. I’ll call the doctor and schedule an appointment for him to look at it tomorrow.” Mom gave me one more hug and made sure I was OK before leaving my room. As I sat on my bed the Evil Ingrown Toenail began laughing again.

I threw a pillow over my foot, hoping it would silence the Toenail's laughter, and allow me to form a plan to defeat it. "You can't silence me, little girl!" the Evil Ingrown Toenail said. "Soon you will sleep and the toe will be mine! Mine, I tell ya, MINE! Muahhahaha!"

The Evil Ingrown Toenail was right! It was late and I was tired. I couldn't keep myself awake for long. I started walking around my room doing all sorts of things to keep myself from falling asleep. "Emma! Bedtime!" shouted Mom from the hall.

No not bedtime! I quickly tried to figure out a way to get out of going to bed. I saw some paints on my desk and quickly spilled some on my head. "Emma are you almost … Oh my goodness, what happened?" Mom said, standing in my doorway.

"Sorry Mom. I accidently bumped into my desk as I was playing on the floor and the paint tipped over and spilled on my head. May I take a shower to get it off?"

I could tell Mom knew I was up to something but she still allowed me to take a shower. "I'll be in your sister's room reading her a story," Mom said. "Come in when you are done."

I went into the bathroom and thought about what I was going to do next.

"Nice move!" the Evil Ingrown Toenail said. "You delayed your bedtime but you can't be in here forever. Sooner or later you WILL be going to bed! Muuhahahhaha!"

His cruel chuckle was really getting to me and I began to give up. I started to cry as I turned on the water and stepped into the shower.

"AHHHH!" The Evil Ingrown toenail shouted in pain as the water hit it. The water was very cold because I forgot to turn the water handle to warm before getting into the shower.

Just then it hit me. Cold hurts him! I turned the water handle all the way to the coldest setting and stood there in the shower as the water filled up the tub, drowning out the cries of the Evil Ingrown Toenail.

I laughed in victory and felt that maybe I could beat him! I began to stomp around the tub laughing and waving my hands around in celebration

Just then, STRIKE! A sharp pain hit my toe. The Evil Ingrown Toenail is getting desperate. It feels as if he's starting to eat my toe! I jumped out of the water in fear, holding my big toe and trying to help prevent the Evil Ingrown Toenail from eating my toe, but I could still feel the pain. The cold water is working but it is not cold enough. What I need is water cold enough to freeze this thing!

ICE! Of course! Oh you're in for it now, Evil Ingrown Toenail! I rushed to the kitchen, grabbing one of Mom's big serving bowls and filled it with ice and water.

"No! You can't! PLEASE DON'T!" The Evil Ingrown Toenail was pleading with me not to, but I just looked at him with a smile on my face and quickly put my foot in the freezing water!

YIKES! It was cold but my voice was nowhere near as loud as the Evil Ingrown Toenail's!

"NOOOOOOOOOOOOOOOOOOOOOOOOOO! AHHHHHHHH!" The Evil Ingrown Toenails screams of pain, soon turned to teeth chattering. At first I thought it was his teeth but then realized the chattering teeth were mine.

It worked! The pain was gone and it seemed as if the Evil Ingrown Toenail's face had disappeared.

"Emma, what on earth are you doing?" Mom had come into the kitchen wondering what all the noise was about.

I wanted to tell Mom everything that had been going on, but she didn't believe me the first time so I quickly formed a plan. I quickly whipped up some tears and said, "Mom my toe was hurting again and I put it in water to make it feel better. I'm scared that if I take it out it will hurt again."

"Oh, Emma," Mom said. She quietly grabbed a towel and put some ice in it and walked me upstairs to my bedroom. She wrapped the towel with ice around my foot and kissed me on the forehead.

"You rest now and you'll see that this will help with the pain," Mom said calmly. "If it begins to hurt again during the night, just call me." I began to relax and could feel my eyelids getting heavy.

I woke up with the sun beating on my face. I looked around and noticed that the towel on my big toe was gone.

I could feel the Evil Ingrown Toenail waking up and I started to panic. I quickly got dressed and was about to go downstairs to wrap my foot again when I heard my mom calling for me.

I found my mom in the kitchen putting her shoes on. “Time to go, Honey. We are off to see Dr. Kohl about your toe,” Mom said.

We were in the car and I could feel the Evil Ingrown Toenail eating away at my big toe. I started to feel dizzy by the time we got to Dr. Kohl’s office.

Dr. Kohl came into the room where I was and could see I was not well. “Emma, I hear your toe is sore.”

I told Dr. Kohl that my toenail was eating my Big Toe and that I ....”

(BLACK OUT!!!)

When I woke up my mom was holding me and Dr. Kohl looked at me, asking if I was OK. I had passed out when talking to him. "Doctor Kohl," I asked, "Is my big toe still there? Did you get rid of the Evil Ingrown Toenail?"

Dr. Kohl smiled and said, "Emma, your big toe is fine. Your nail happened to have grown a little bit in the side of your toe, which was giving you some pain. I clipped it out and put some medicine on it to help it heal."

I could see he had put a nice pink band aid on it and I wiggled my toes, happy that the Evil Ingrown Toenail was gone!

So remember if you EVER get an EVIL Ingrown Toenail, use ice! It's a great weapon. Oh, and I passed my belt test. You are now looking at a happy Black Belt! My name is Emma and I thank you for listening.

www.ingramcontent.com/pod-product-compliance
Lightning Source LLC
Chambersburg PA
CBHW080810020826
48982CB00018B/1018

* 9 7 8 0 9 8 8 7 4 6 3 1 2 *